Barbie it Takes Two

FRIENDS FOREVER

studio fun
INTERNATIONAL

Barbie from Brooklyn and Barbie from Malibu were sitting together in the kitchen, ready to try the newest culinary creation Brooklyn's dad had made, when Brooklyn's mom arrived home from work. She mentioned that there had been some fancy, first-class VIP on her flight.

"His name had something to do with a bird . . . Otto Pheasant . . ." she said.

"Otto PHOENIX?!" asked Brooklyn.
"As in world-renowned, star-making, TV and music media mogul Otto Phoenix?!" asked Malibu.

The two girls knew they just had to meet him. If they could perform in front of him, their dreams of becoming famous would definitely come true!

The next day at school, Brooklyn and Malibu told Rafa about their idea.

"Girls, there's no way you can get a meeting with Otto Phoenix . . . He's not just famous. He's like famous to famous people famous," Rafa said.

"Which is why we have a flawless plan," said Malibu. Brooklyn pulled out a tablet from her backpack.

She ran through Otto's schedule, which included three crystal meditation breaks.

"And once they're cleared, it's the perfect time to swoop right in!" Malibu explained.

With their perfect plan in place, the girls went to Otto Phoenix's office and asked his assistant, Pandora, to get them an appointment with Mr. Phoenix.

Pandora was nice enough to get them a meeting with him . . . in *seven years!*

Brooklyn and Malibu were disappointed, but they wouldn't give up that easily! The girls knew they couldn't go back without Pandora recognizing them. They needed disguises!

Pretending to be members of a girl band, Brooklyn and Malibu arrived and requested a meeting with Mr. Phoenix using their best British accents. Pandora checked her calendar and gave them a new appointment, but it wasn't for eight years!

The two friends couldn't wait seven or eight years to follow their dreams! So Brooklyn and Malibu continued to come back in disguise after disguise, but nothing they did worked. Pandora always knew it was them, and she wouldn't let them near Mr. Phoenix anytime soon.

Finally, the girls had the perfect plan. Brooklyn and Malibu would dress up in fruit costumes and arrive with a smoothie delivery for Mr. Phoenix. They were sure their plan would work this time. Pandora would be so impressed by their creativity and determination, she would have to let them meet with Mr. Phoenix!

When they arrived with the smoothie, their plan
was thwarted almost immediately.

"Otto's on a strict, soft pretzel-only diet . . . but
I'm not," said Pandora. She took the smoothie from
Brooklyn and took a big gulp. Then she stood up
and once again sent the girls away. Pandora was not
messing around!

Back at Brooklyn's house, the girls were struggling to come up with a new plan. In the kitchen, her twin neighbors, Jackson and Jayla, were helping Brooklyn's dad make his newest kitchen creation: *taralli*—the Italian version of a soft pretzel.

That gave Brooklyn and Malibu an idea.

"Dad, how would you like to make a batch of those for Otto Phoenix?" Brooklyn asked.

They knew Otto loved soft pretzels, so if they brought a freshly made batch of taralli to his office, Pandora would definitely let them meet Mr. Phoenix. This plan was foolproof!

Brooklyn's dad agreed to help them. He, Jackson, and Jayla worked together to try and make a perfect batch of pretzels for Mr. Phoenix. Brooklyn's dad worked late into the night, and even tried to get their cat, Etta, to try one of his batters.

The next morning, Brooklyn and Malibu found him asleep on the kitchen counter. He had made the perfect batch of taralli!

Their plan was officially in motion. Before they arrived at the office, Brooklyn and Malibu put on cute cat masks that Rafa had made them. Then, with freshly made pretzels in hand, they walked into Mr. Phoenix's office and asked Pandora for a meeting. Today was going to be their lucky day!

Brooklyn and Malibu eagerly waited for Pandora to give them the good news.

"Otto refuses to taste anything unless it goes through several rigorous quality control tests, so . . . lucky me," said Pandora as she took the box and helped herself to one of the pretzels.

The girls were devastated. Their perfect plan had been foiled once again!

"It's hopeless. Nothing gets past Pandora. She's like an indestructible concrete wall . . ." Brooklyn said once they were outside.

As they walked out, Malibu looked up at Mr. Phoenix's building. She saw that there was a crew working to clean all of the windows. Suddenly, she had an idea that was sure to work!

"But if we had a window . . ." Malibu said with a smile.

Soon, Brooklyn and Malibu were scaling the outside of the building on a window cleaner's platform!

"I can't believe you talked me into this," said Brooklyn as they were hoisted higher and higher above the ground. Now they just needed to find Mr. Phoenix's window.

Finally, Brooklyn and Malibu found the right window. As they peered through Mr. Phoenix's window, they saw . . . Pandora! She spotted them right away and, with a smile on her face, quickly closed the blinds.

Disappointed, Brooklyn and Malibu headed back down the side of the building.

"All this disappointment is making me hungry," said Brooklyn once they were back on the ground.
The girls found a nearby pretzel cart. Just as they finished ordering, someone else walked up to the cart.

"Hey, Sammy, heavy on the mustard today. My energy flow needs a boost," the man said.
"Sorry, boss. These girls ahead of you got the last one," the vendor replied.
Malibu and Brooklyn turned around and saw it was Otto Phoenix!

"You're . . . him!" exclaimed Brooklyn.
"And you two are Barbie Roberts . . . I saw
your performance. The Spotlight Showcase
in Times Square. Send me your stuff, then we
should talk," he said, handing them his card.
"Stuff it is! Coming your way!" said Brooklyn.

Bursting with excitement, the girls raced back to Brooklyn's house.

"We met Otto Phoenix!" Brooklyn announced.

"It was the pretzels, wasn't it?" Brooklyn's dad asked.

"You could say that," said Malibu with a smile.

"Well, that's good, because there's a lot more where those came from!" he said as Jackson and Jayla walked in carrying trays of giant pretzels.